This Book Belongs to:

D1495937

Did you ever have that moment where you felt things couldn't get any worse & you needed something or someone to make it all get better? Well, that's exactly the spirit of The Flyin Lion. 'Leon' was created by my dad when I experienced a complication during the recovery of my first surgery at the age of two. I had just undergone a surgical fusion of the top two vertebrae in my cervical spine to prevent paralysis, which can occur all too often with my type of skeletal dysplasia. My at home recovery involved stabilization of my neck with a "halo" cast. Well, as you might expect a two year old to do, I was screaming and crying out in protest and resisting my medicine and I dislodged the two front screws that held my halo in place to my skull. Panic struck and we rushed by ambulance to the hospital to try to avoid serious damage to my spine. My dad, with creativity, calm, and brilliance took a small stuffed animal 'lion' I had and during the ambulance ride started singing this song to comfort me:

> *I'm a Flyin Lion, you'll never catch me cryin'.*
> *When things go wrong I just sing my song,*
> *And it makes me strong,*
> *Because I'm a Flyin Lion,*
> *You'll never catch me cryin'....*

As my father flew my little lion around me, I calmed down enough to get to the hospital and allow my doctors to care for me. On that day, The Flyin Lion was born! He would reappear many more times over the years to protect and accompany me for multiple surgeries that were still to come. Now my dad is spreading the spirit of The Flyin Lion to my children, his grand children; Will & Zoey with stories to help them cope with tough times and learn lessons of hope, empowerment, caring, and family traditions. I hope that every parent who has ever struggled to quiet an upset child will find comfort in these stories of The Flyin Lion. I know Will and Zoey love to sit with their Grand Ba (as named by Will his first grandchild) and learn these entertaining life lessons large and small. Today I'm so pleased that many more children may benefit from this gift that my dad gave to me when I was young and needed someone to make things better.
Welcome to the magic of The Flyin Lion.

Jennifer Arnold, M.D.

Flyin' Lion
& Friends

Shooting Star

CITATION MEDIA

Foreword: Jennifer Arnold, M.D.

Written By: David Arnold

Illustrations: Erin C. McCrea

I'm a Flyin' Lion,
You'll never catch me cryin….
When things go wrong,
I just sing my song and
It makes me strong,
Cause I'm a Flyin' Lion,
I'll always keep on smilin'
Cause I'm a Flyin' Lion,
I'll always keep on tryin'
You'll NEVER catch me cryin!

Sometimes at dusk,
as daylight leaves the sky,
I gaze out my window and
wonder why
Looking up oh so high,
the sun it had to go to bed.

It's like the world lets out a sigh,
And whispers to me, "It's not goodbye."
So here we are at the end of the day,
And now's the time for stars to play.

Across the sky we twinkle light,
Some red, some blue, but most are white.
It's like we dance across the night,
For the moon so big and bright.

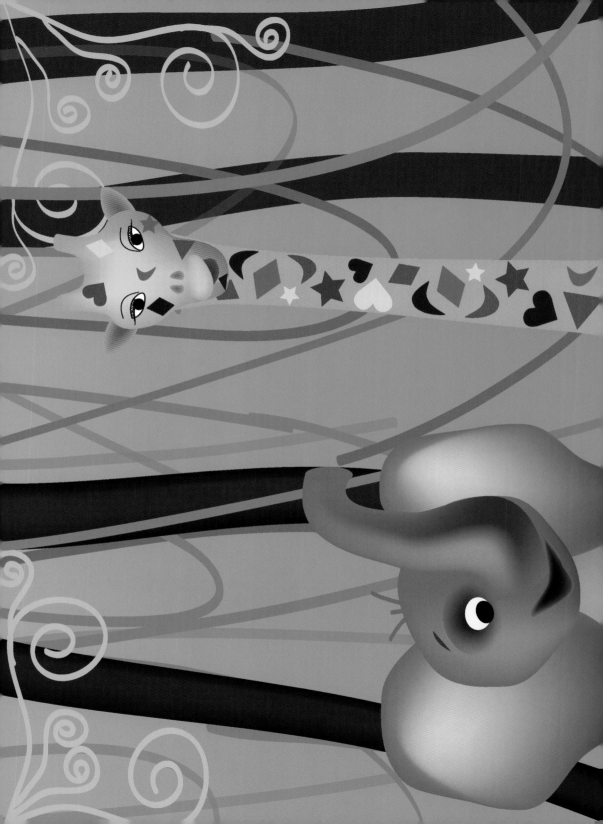

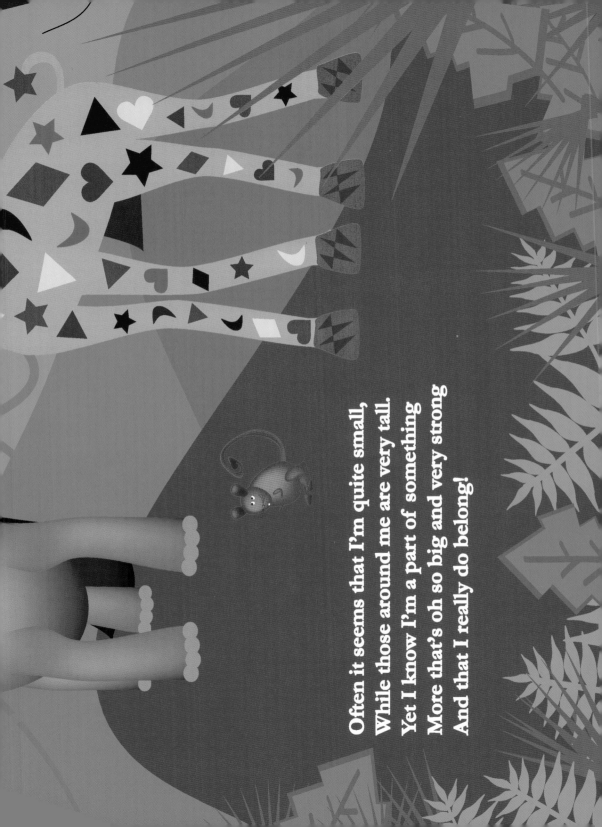

Often it seems that I'm quite small,
While those around me are very tall.
Yet I know I'm a part of something
More that's oh so big and very strong
And that I really do belong!

On those nights while being still
and gazing past my window sill,

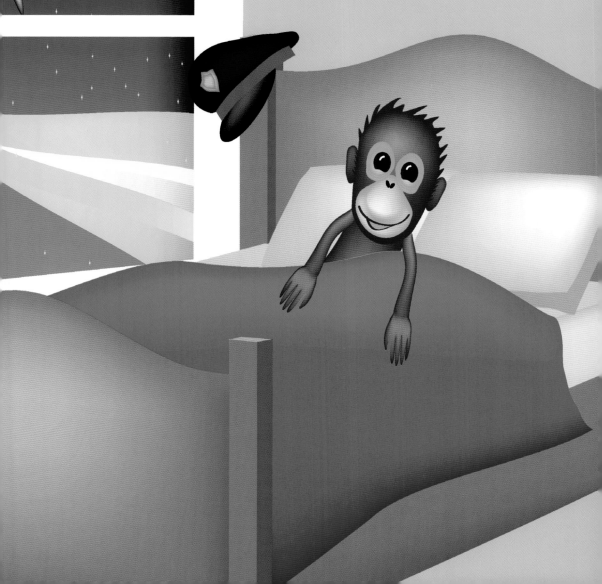

I sometimes see a shooting star
that could be me or could be you,
can you see it where you are?

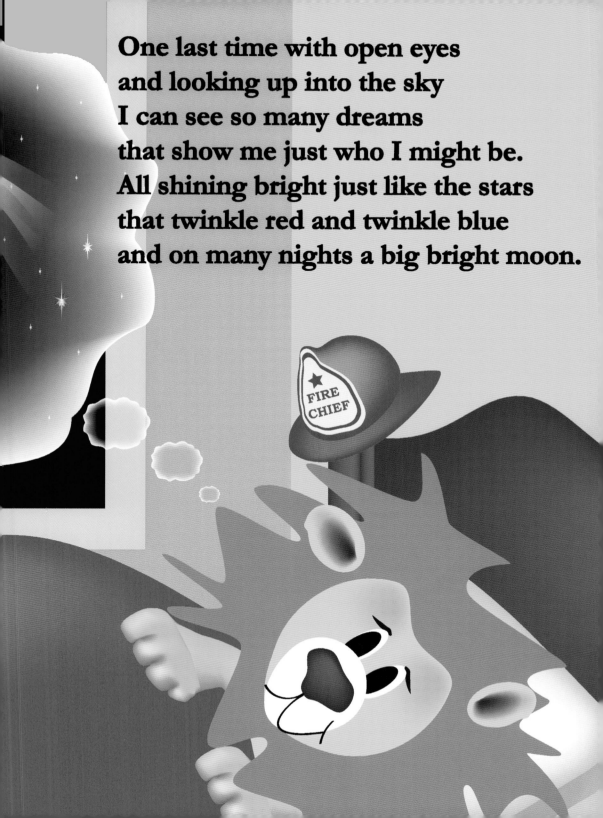

One last time with open eyes
and looking up into the sky
I can see so many dreams
that show me just who I might be.
All shining bright just like the stars
that twinkle red and twinkle blue
and on many nights a big bright moon.

FIRE
CHIEF

So as the minutes pass and I get closer
to that time to say good night,
I try my best to put sleep off
and so I often count star lights.
1, 2, 3, 4, 5, 6, 7 –
There are so many up in the heavens.

Tick...Tock..

Tick...Tock..

Tick...Tock..

Tick...Tock..

Roar...

Zzzz...

Yet, I usually never last too long, so sound asleep here in my room is where you'll find me all too soon.

Roar...

Zzzz...

Or even as I'm lying still I can dream a dream so bright that my glow lights up my bedroom just like the stars light up the night.

ABCDEFGHIJKLMNOPQRSTUVWXYZ

Bat, bat
Cat, cat
Hat, hat

$1 + 1 = 2$
$2 + 2 = 4$

Be a Do Gooder to Someone Today!

Each of us, we are important in this big world. So be a friend to others and yourself while reaching for your dream by learning, doing and going places some of which you're yet to see.

So just before you fall asleep,
here's a thought for you to keep,
a secret we can share.

That you and I, we're a lot alike,
and all that really matters is we dare
to shine our light and show we care!

Across the sky we twinkle light,
some red, some blue, but most are white.

It's like we dance across the night,
for the moon so big and bright!

So go ahead and reach for your
dreams, it's really not that far,

You have to go to be a star,
and all that you might hope
for and dream this dream
while you're asleep!

Imagine you're the brightest light that shines for all to see and twinkles red or maybe blue, sometimes like a big white moon.

And you'll
Be dreaming
The same
As me!

TOYS

Flyin' Lion and his friends all catching their own dreams as they zoom across the sky inviting you to always do your best at everything you try!

Flyin' Lion and Friends

Soar Caring

Leon
Strong Leader

Mandi
Curious

Mortimer Wise

Zippy
Respectful

Elsa
Dependable

Harley Loyal

Do-Gooders Club

Twee Courageous

Stretch
Patient

Gigi
Positive

Blinky Kind

Zoey Smart

Shhh
Creative

Al Courteous

Who are you most like?

Leon the Flyin Lion and Friends hope you enjoy this bedtime story!

A portion of the proceeds from this book will be donated to the
Angels in Adoption® Program (AIA) to help support their
Important work on behalf of the author's grandchildren;
William Rijin Klein * Zoey Nidhi Klein * Nathan David Arnold

AIA is a part of the Congressional Coalition on Adoption Institute
A nonprofit, nonpartisan organization dedicated to raising
Awareness about the millions of children around the world in
Need of permanent, safe, and loving homes and to eliminating
The barriers that hinder these children from realizing their basic
Right of a family.

CCAI's Vision is a world in which every child
Knows the love and support of a family.

CONGRESSIONAL COALITION ON ADOPTION INSTITUTE

You can learn more about CCAI & AIA by visiting their websites:
ccainstitute.org or angelsinadoption.org

Citation Media
For Inquiries, call 845-469-8605

Copyright 2018 Citation Media
Published by Citation Media LLC
91 Odyssey Drive
Chester, NY 10918

Printed in China

ISBN-10: 0-9992986-0-7
ISBN-13: 978-0-9992986-0-2
1C M18 1

CEO Charlotte Bonhard

Author
David Arnold

Illustrations
Erin C. McCrea

CITATION MEDIA